# FROGGY GETS DRESSED

# FROGGY GETS DRESSED

by JONATHAN LONDON
illustrated by FRANK REMKIEWICZ

SCHOLASTIC INC.
New York Toronto London Auckland Sydney

**For Sean & Aaron**
**who love the snow**
**—J.L.**

**For Madeleine**
**—F.R.**



ISBN 0-590-73600-0

 Published by Scholastic Inc., 555 Broadway, New York, NY 10012, by arrangement with Penguin Books USA Inc.

12 11 10 9 8 7 6 5 4 3 2 6 7 8 9/9 0/0

Printed in the U.S.A. 14

First Scholastic printing, December 1995

It was cold.
Froggy woke up
and looked out the window.
"Snow! Snow!" he sang.
"I want to play in the snow!"

"Go back to sleep, Froggy,"
said his mother.
"Don't you know?
Frogs are supposed to sleep
all winter. Wake up
when the snow melts."

“No! No!” cried Froggy.
“I’m awake! Awake!
I want to go out and play
in the snow.”

So Froggy put on his socks—*zoop!*

Pulled on his boots—*zup!*

Put on his hat—*zat!*

Tied on his scarf—*zwit!*

Tugged on his mittens—*zum!*

And flopped outside

into the snow—*flop flop flop.*

FRRROOGGYY!

called his mother.

**"Wha-a-a-a-t?"**

yelled Froggy.

"Did you forget

to put something on?"

Froggy looked down.
"Oops!" cried Froggy. "I forgot
to put on my pants!"

He flopped back inside—*flop flop flop.*

Tugged off his mittens.

Untied his scarf.

Took off his hat.

Pulled off his boots

(he left his socks on)

and slipped his pants on—*zip!*

Then he pulled on his boots—*zup!*

Put on his hat—*zat!*

Tied on his scarf—*zwit!*

Tugged on his mittens—*zum!*

And flopped back outside
into the snow—*flop flop flop.*

FRRROOGGYY!

called his mother.

**"Wha-a-a-a-t?"**

yelled Froggy.

"Did you forget

to put something on?"

Froggy looked down.
"Oops!" he cried. "I forgot
to put on my shirt!"

"*And* your coat!" added his mother.

He flopped back inside—*flop flop flop.*

Tugged off his mittens.

Untied his scarf.

Took off his hat

(he left his pants,

boots, and socks on)

and buttoned up

his shirt—*zut! zut! zut!*

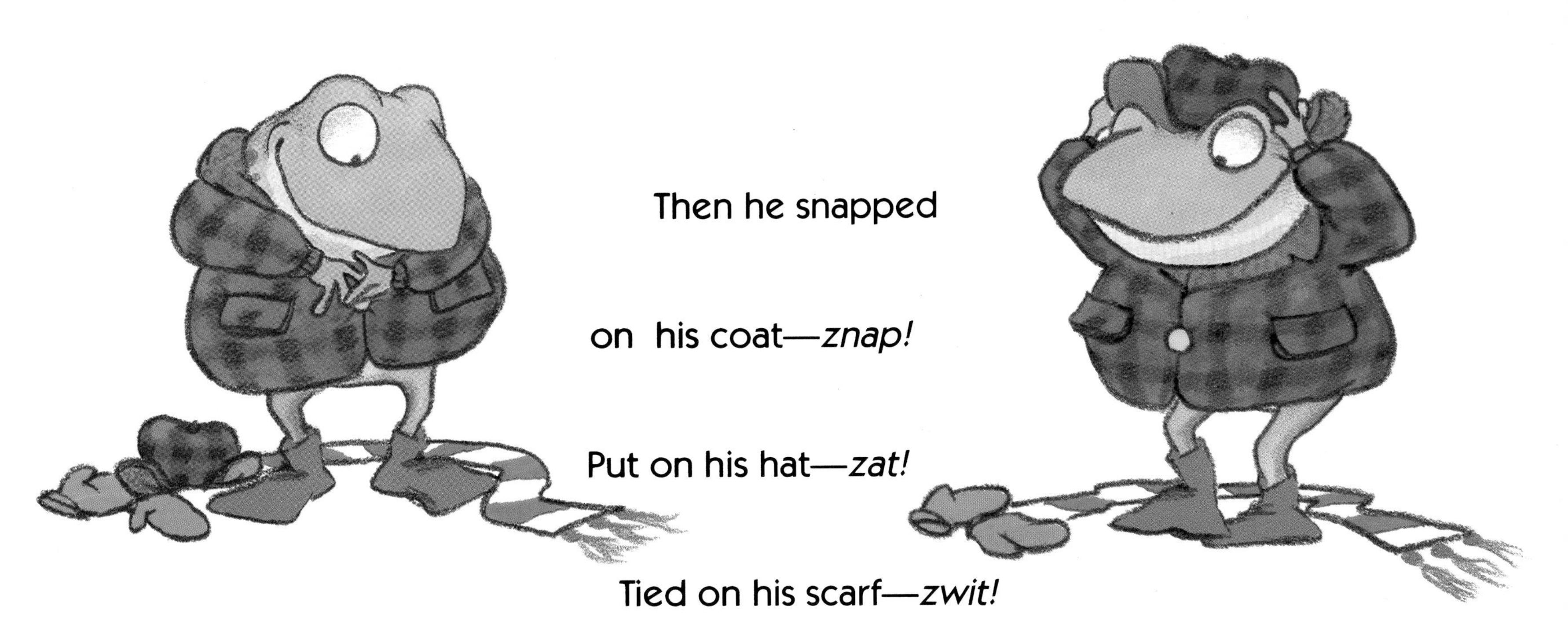

Then he snapped

on his coat—*znap!*

Put on his hat—*zat!*

Tied on his scarf—*zwit!*

Tugged on his mittens—*zum!*

And flopped back outside

into the snow—*flop flop flop.*

FRRROOGGYY!

called his mother.

**"Wha-a-a-a-t?"**

yelled Froggy.

"Did you forget to
put something on?"

Froggy looked down.
He had on his mittens.
He had on his scarf.
He had on his coat.
He had on his shirt.
He had on his pants.
He had on his boots.
He had on his socks.
He reached up—
Yep! He had on his hat.
What could be missing?

His mother laughed.

"Oops!" cried Froggy,
looking more red in the face
than green.

He flopped back inside—*flop flop flop.*

Tugged off his mittens.

Untied his scarf.

Unsnapped his coat.

Unbuttoned his shirt.

Unzipped his pants.

Pulled off his boots.

Took off his socks

(he left his hat on)

and slipped his long johns on—

with a *zap!* of elastic.

Then he put on one sock—*zoop!*

Pulled on one boot—*zup!*

Tugged on one mitten—*zum!*

Started to tug on the other...

...and let it drop.

And said, "I'm too tired."

And went back to sleep.

ZZZZZZzzz
GOOD NIGHT
FROGGY